This Book Belongs to:

THE FAT ROUND BROWN HOUND

by Sally Mayer

Tate Publishing & Enterprises

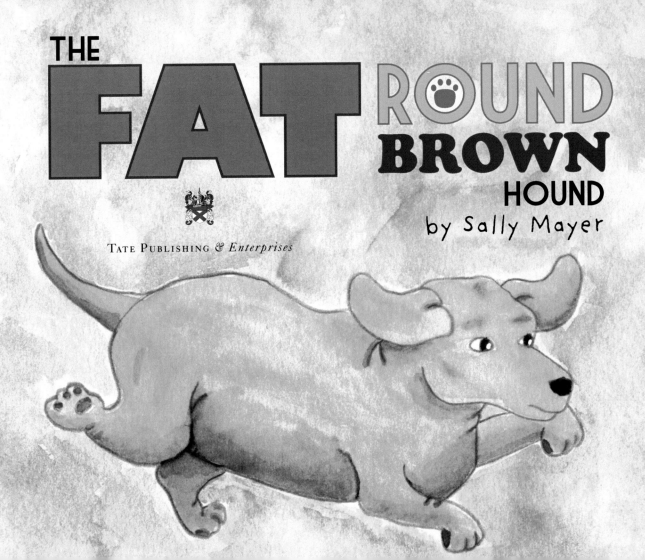

Published by Tate Publishing & Enterprises, LLC
127 E. Trade Center Terrace | Mustang, Oklahoma 73064 USA
1.888.361.9473 | www.tatepublishing.com

Tate Publishing is committed to excellence in the publishing industry. The company reflects the philosophy established by the founders, based on Psalm 68:11,
"The Lord gave the word and great was the company of those who published it."

Book design copyright © 2008 by Tate Publishing, LLC. All rights reserved.
*Cover and Interior design by Eddie Russell_*
Illustration by Katie Brooks

Published in the United States of America

ISBN: 978-1-60696-928-1
1. Juvenile Fiction: Animals:Dogs: 0-5
2. Youth and Children: Children: General: 0-5
08.10.28

Dedicated to My Family
and to the Memory of Betty Lou

The round brown hound lives with two nice ladies in the country. She loves the big green fields because she thinks it is fun to run. The round brown hound also likes to dig holes and climb in them. She loves to pick the ripest blackberries from the bushes with her sharp teeth. And sometimes she just lies back and basks in the sun. She especially loves to eat.

But one thing that the round brown hound does not like is water. The round brown hound *hates* water!

Now she is running to play by the river with her friends, Peelio, Dotty, and Betty Lou. They are having a wonderful time playing with a stick. Soon, they get tired. "I have an idea," barks Dotty. "Let's go swimming and cool off in the water!"

"Yeah, let's go!" yelp all the other dogs, but not the round brown hound. After all, the round brown hound hates water.

"But none of us knows how to swim," she whines.

"Well, how hard can it be?" asks Dotty. "Come on guys!" she calls as she struts into the water.

The round brown hound digs a hole to hide in. "I hate water," she grumbles.

"I don't know, you guys," woofs Betty Lou. "I think I'll stay here on the shore where it's safe."

So Dotty and Peelio swim out alone. Dotty swims much faster than Peelio. Soon Peelio starts to panic. "Help! My paw is caught on something! I'm sinking! *Help!*" he shrieks, but Dotty is too far away to help him.

Betty Lou runs to help, but trips and hurts her ankle. It's all up to the round brown hound now! She gathers up all of her courage and jumps down from her hole. "I'm coming, Peelio!" she yells as she runs down the bank and into the water.

Peelio has almost sunk below the water's surface, and she has to dive under to find him. He's caught on some river grass! The round brown hound chews through the plant with her sharp teeth and frees Peelio.

Dotty swims over and helps Peelio back to shore. Peelio is so grateful to the round brown hound that he gives her a big, wet, doggy kiss! "Well, you saved the day," says Dotty to the round brown hound. "The round brown hound is a hero!"

The friends all return home together and tell the two nice ladies the story of how the round brown hound saved Peelio. They are all so proud of her because they know how much she hates water. The two nice ladies cook lots of food and have a party in her honor. She eats and eats and eats and...

.

...and that is the story of how she became the *fat* round brown hound!

The End

The fat round brown hound now resides in the countryside of southern Maryland with the two nice ladies. She is slimmer now and has experienced many more adventures, but those are stories for another day...

e|LIVE

---

listen|imagine|view|experience

AUDIO BOOK DOWNLOAD INCLUDED WITH THIS BOOK!

In your hands you hold a complete digital entertainment package. Besides purchasing the paper version of this book, this book includes a free download of the audio version of this book. Simply use the code listed below when visiting our website. Once downloaded to your computer, you can listen to the book through your computer's speakers, burn it to an audio CD or save the file to your portable music device (such as Apple's popular iPod) and listen on the go!

How to get your free audio book digital download:

1. Visit www.tatepublishing.com and click on the e|LIVE logo on the home page.
2. Enter the following coupon code:
   b59c-5c56-0f1a-f835-4002-7b6a-9d06-61f2
3. Download the audio book from your e|LIVE digital locker and begin enjoying your new digital entertainment package today!